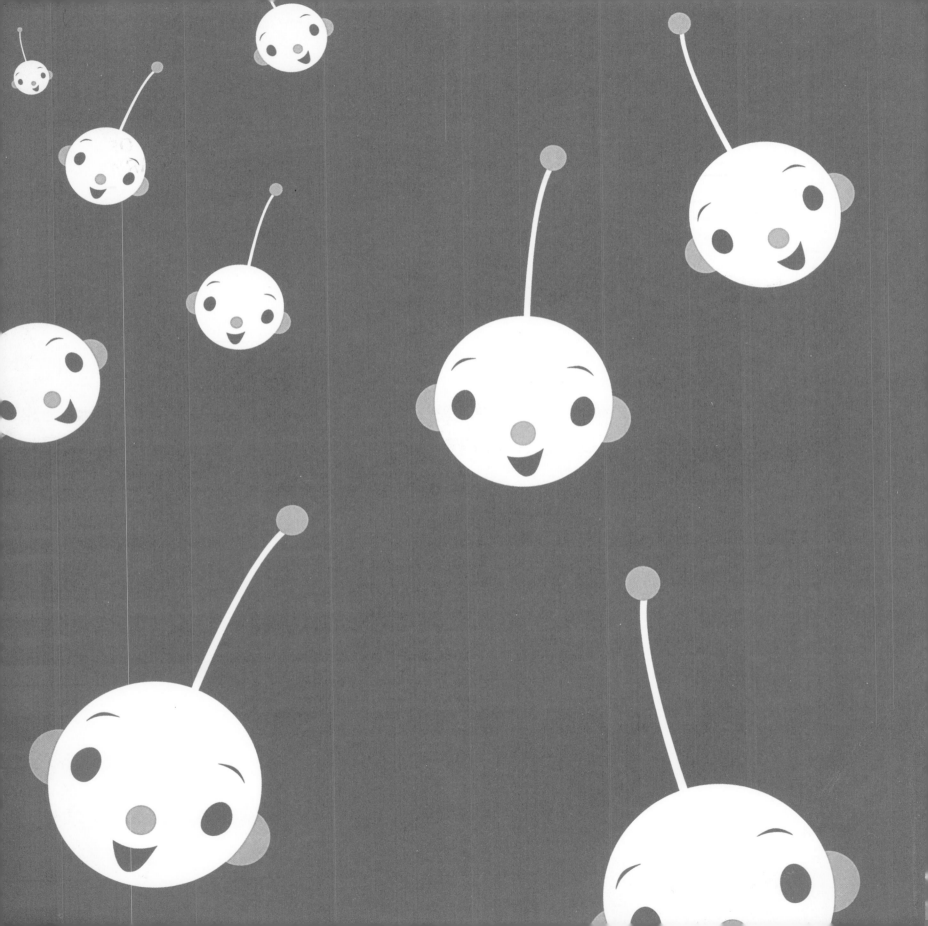

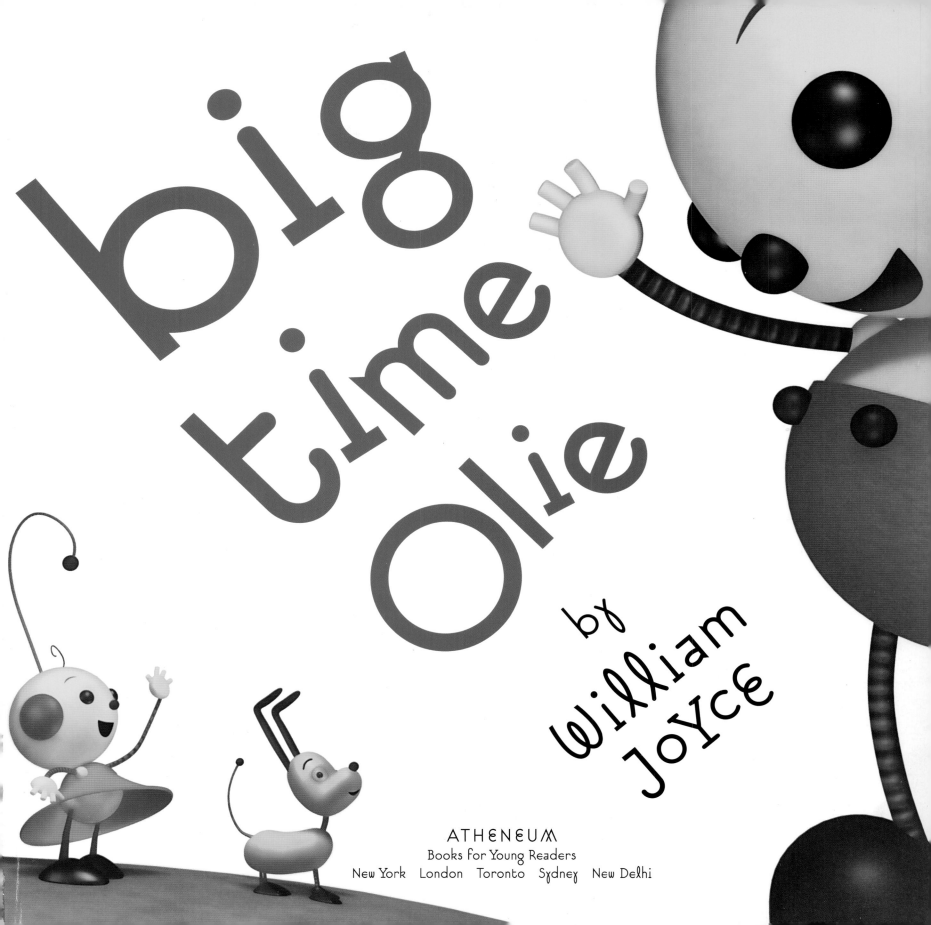

big time Olie

by William Joyce

ATHENEUM
Books for Young Readers
New York   London   Toronto   Sydney   New Delhi

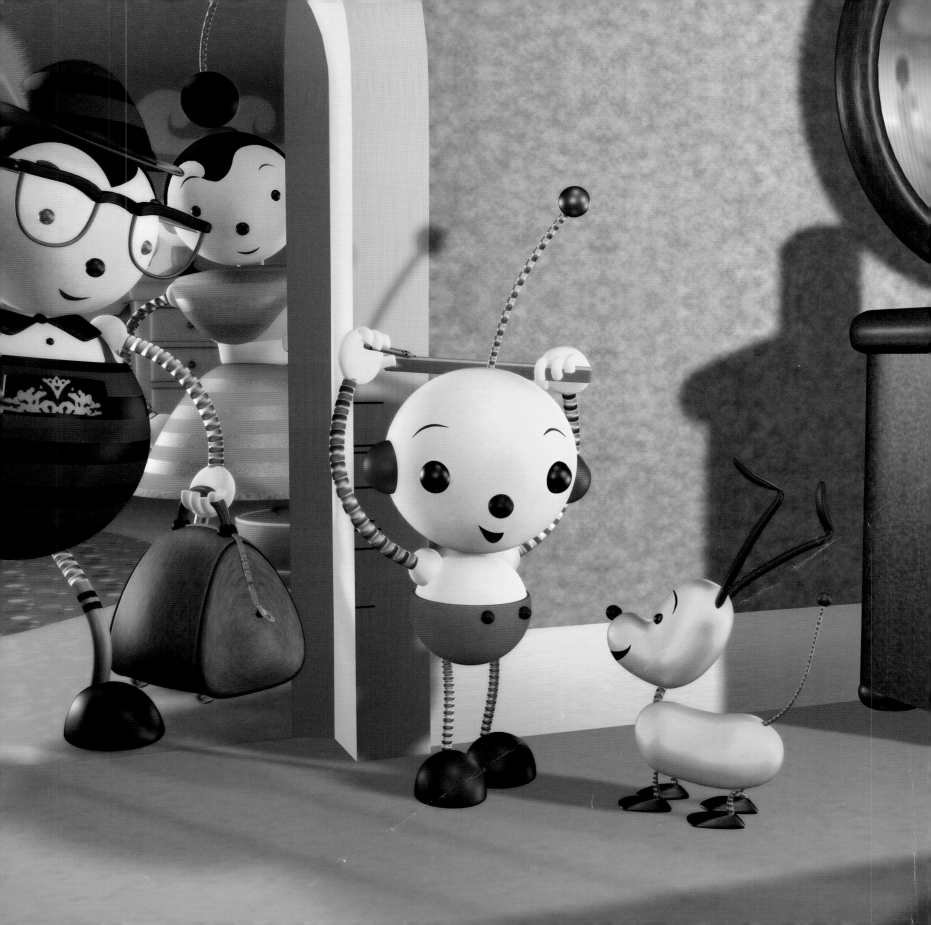

Rolie Polie Olie was sizing up quite nicely.

In fact, he grew a little bigger every day.

He even sang a song about it.

I'm a little bit bigger,
not a little bit smaller.
I'm a little bit taller—
I'm growing Rolie up!"

But when Mom and Dad took a trip to Mount Big Ball, they said Olie was too little to go—

which Olie thought was big time unfair!

Then Pappy said he was too big
to jump on his bed
while eating ice cream.
So Olie shouted in his biggest voice,

"I'M NOT
THE RIGHT
SIZE FOR
ANYTHING!"

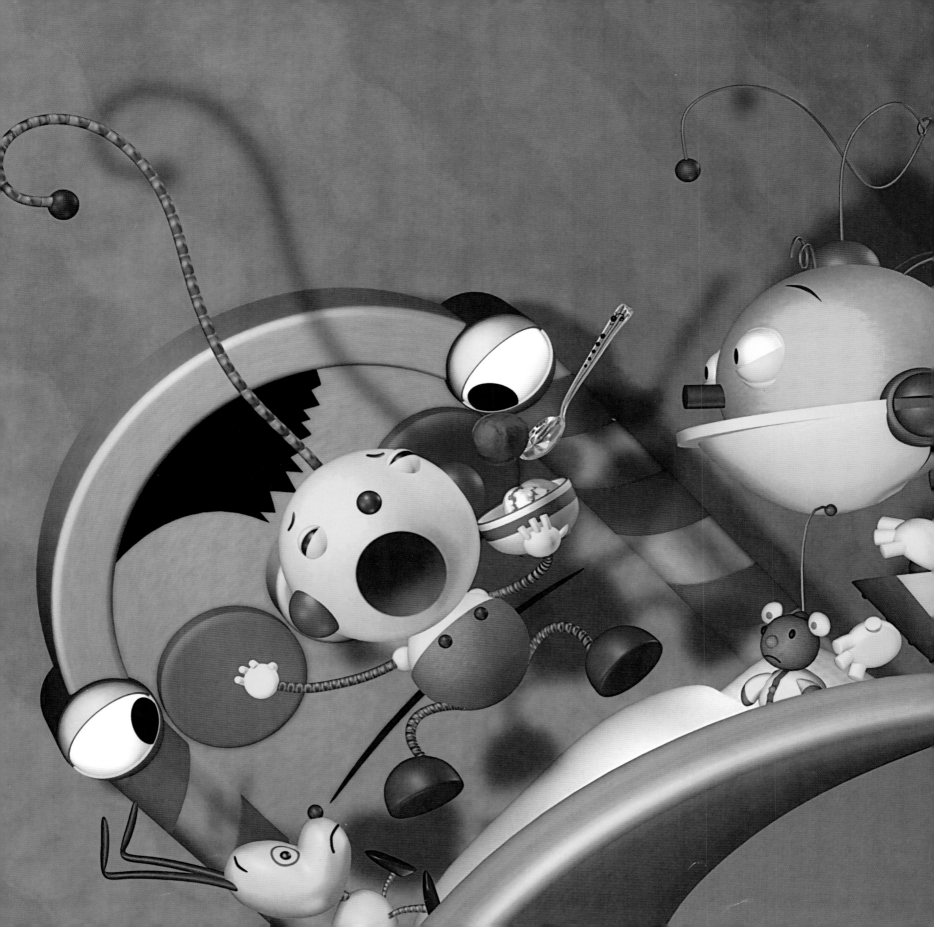

He was so unhappy.

He got a big and really bad idea.

He would use the shrink-and-grow-a-lator!

He twirled the dial.

He pulled the lever.

He pushed the button—

the wrong button.

He was in a little bit of trouble.

Zowie thought he was a dolly.

But Spot became
a Rolie rescue doggy!

Then Olie pushed the bigger button reeeally hard.

Now that I'm grown up," he said,
"I'll do just what I want."

So he jumped . . .

all the way into outer space,
where he got a scoop of ice cream
from the ice cream planet.

and landed with a big

KABOOM!

He began to sing
in his tiniest voice,

"I'm stuck on top of Mount Big Ball.
I'm lost and lonely and so tall.
I wish I could be back small.
I feel a little sad."

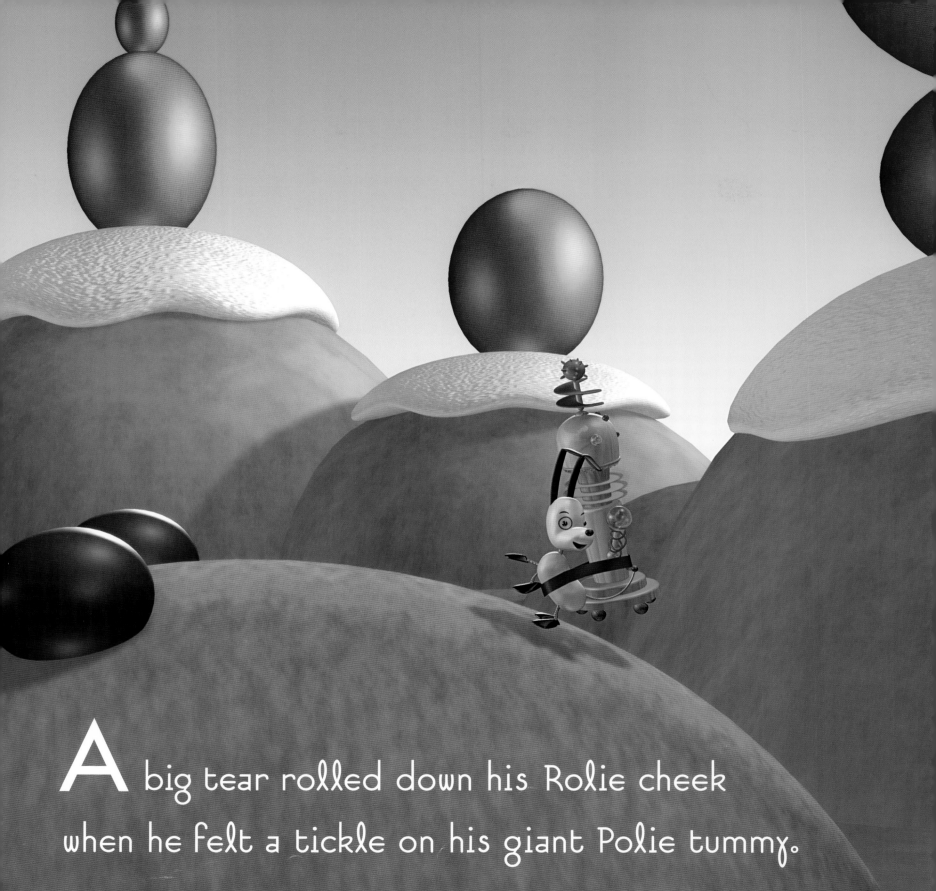

A big tear rolled down his Rolie cheek
when he felt a tickle on his giant Polie tummy.

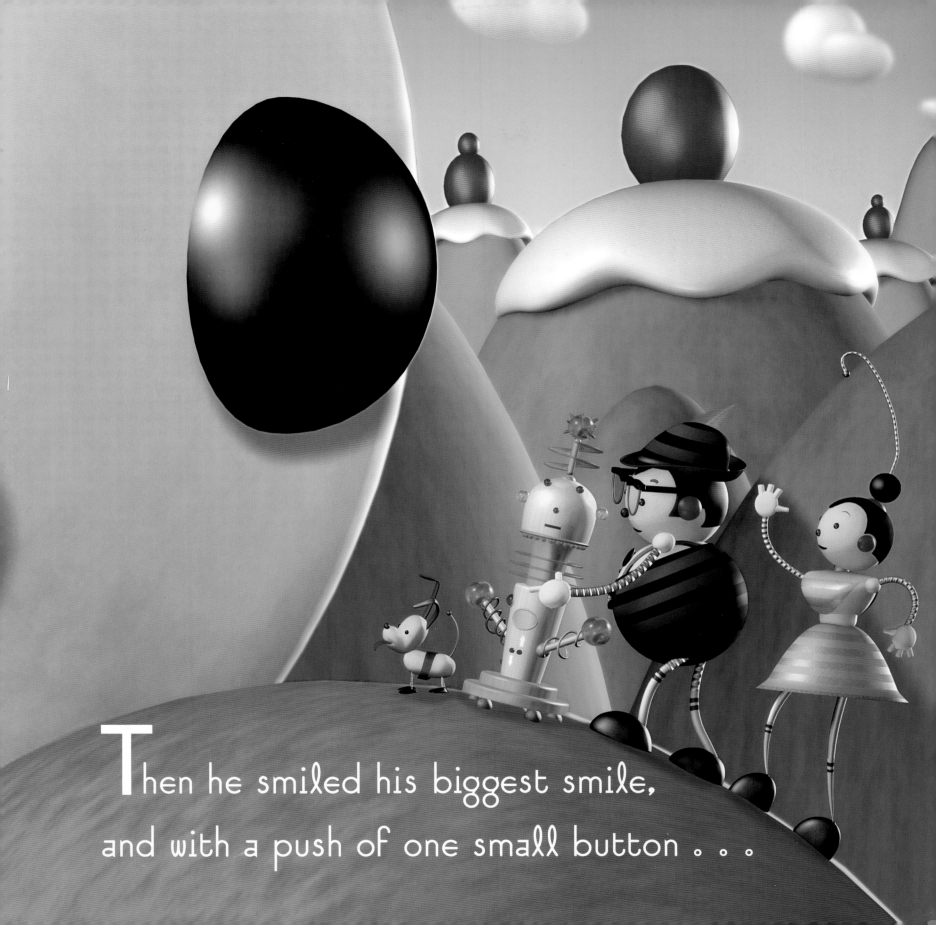

Then he smiled his biggest smile,
and with a push of one small button . . .

he went back to being just plain Olie!

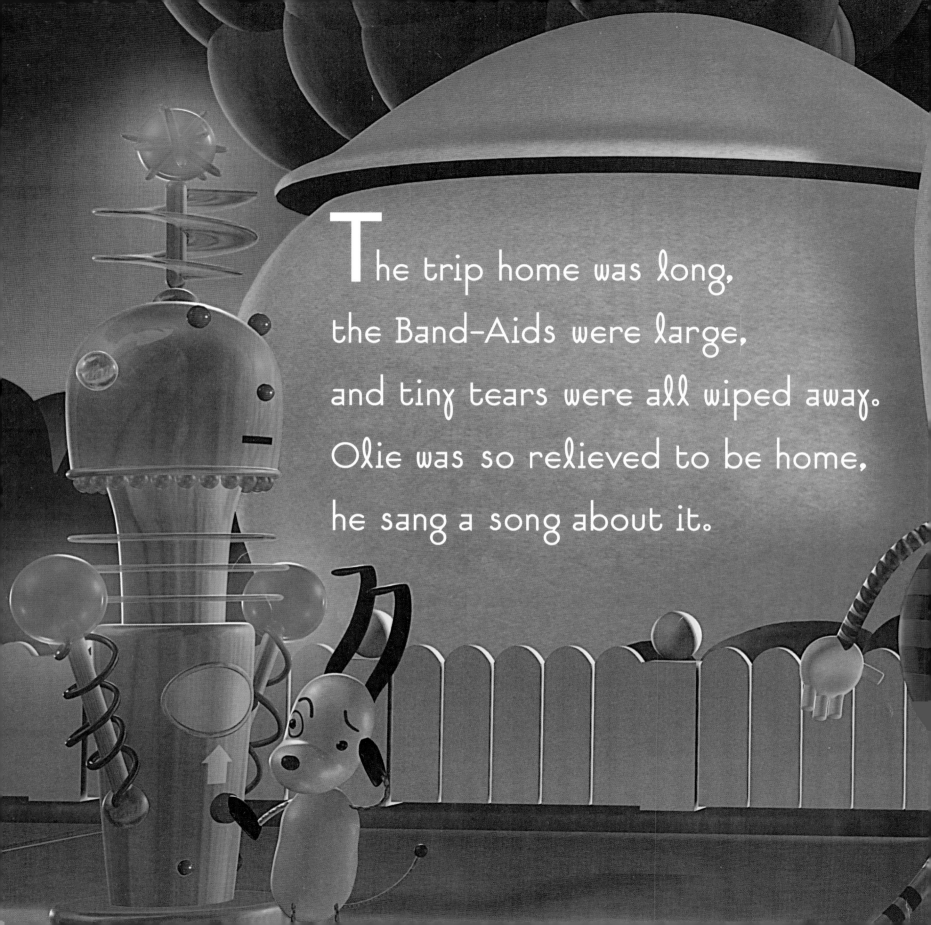

The trip home was long,
the Band-Aids were large,
and tiny tears were all wiped away.
Olie was so relieved to be home,
he sang a song about it.

I was a sorry, sad Olie.
I've been a mad and bad Polie.
I won't be in such a hurry
to grow all Rolie up!"

Then he gave everybody
a big hug and a big kiss,
and he went to sleep
in his bed that was just big enough . . .

for now.

For
Big Time
Rich

Special thanks to
the usual suspects: Pam Lehn,
Susie Grondin, Jordan Thistlewood,
Paul Cieniuch, Gavin Boyle, Ian
MacLeod, Brian Harris, Daniel Abramovich,
Dave Simmons, Kelly Brennan, Don Kim,
Sara Newman, Lisa Kelly, Alicia Mikles, Neil
Swaab, Dorothy Pietrewicz, Ruiko Tokunaga,
Tamar Brazis, Maria Lake, Emily Clark,
Trish Farnsworth, Katie Dunkleman,
and Laura Geringer.

𝒜
atheneum

ATHENEUM BOOKS FOR YOUNG READERS

An imprint of Simon & Schuster Children's Publishing Division

1230 Avenue of the Americas, New York, New York 10020

Text copyright © 2002 by William Joyce • Illustrations copyright © 2002 by Nelvana
Limited. • All rights reserved. Artwork reprinted by permission of Nelvana Limited.
Originally published in 2002 by Laura Geringer Books/HarperCollins Publishers.
ATHENEUM BOOKS FOR YOUNG READERS is a registered trademark of Simon & Schuster, Inc.
Atheneum logo is a trademark of Simon & Schuster, Inc. • For information about special discounts
for bulk purchases, please contact Simon & Schuster Special Sales at 1-866-506-1949 or
business@simonandschuster.com. • The Simon & Schuster Speakers Bureau can bring authors
to your live event. For more information or to book an event, contact the Simon & Schuster
Speakers Bureau at 1-866-248-3049 or visit our website at www.simonspeakers.com.
Book design by Alicia Mikles • The text for this book was set in Rollie Suburban.
The illustrations for this book were digitally rendered. • Manufactured in China • 0118
SCP • First Atheneum Books for Young Readers Edition
2 4 6 8 10 9 7 5 3 1
CIP data for this book is available from the Library of Congress.
ISBN 978-1-4814-8969-0
ISBN 978-1-4814-8970-6 (eBook)